Mom Tiger's New Job

Adapted by Alexandra Cassel Schwartz
Based on the screenplay "Daniel Finds Something to Do"
written by Becky Friedman
Poses and layouts by Jason Fruchter

Simon Spotlight
New York London Toronto Sydney New Delhi

SIMON SPOTLIGHT
An imprint of Simon & Schuster Children's Publishing Division
1230 Avenue of the Americas, New York, New York 10020
This Simon Spotlight paperback edition December 2019
© 2019 The Fred Rogers Company
All rights reserved, including the right of reproduction in whole or in part in any form.
SIMON SPOTLIGHT and colophon are registered trademarks of Simon & Schuster, Inc.
For information about special discounts for bulk purchases, please contact Simon & Schuster
Special Sales at 1-866-506-1949 or business@simonandschuster.com.
Manufactured in the United States of America 1119 LAK
10 9 8 7 6 5 4 3 2 1
ISBN 978-1-5344-5347-0 (pbk)
ISBN 978-1-5344-5348-7 (eBook)

It was a beautiful day in the neighborhood. Daniel was pretending to be a chef in a restaurant.

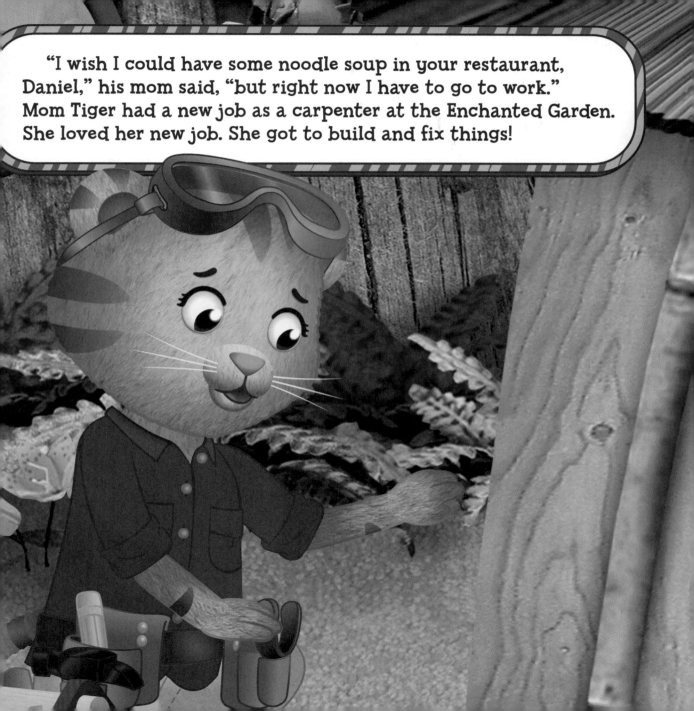

"I wish I could have some noodle soup in your restaurant, Daniel," his mom said, "but right now I have to go to work." Mom Tiger had a new job as a carpenter at the Enchanted Garden. She loved her new job. She got to build and fix things!

"Work?" Daniel asked. "But I want you to play with me!"

"I know," said his mom, "but remember how we talked about my new job? And since Dad and Margaret are out, I need you to come to work with me."

Daniel wanted to go to work with his mom. But he was nervous. "But if you're working, what will I do?" Daniel asked.

Mom told Daniel to look around for something to take with him to the Enchanted Garden. She sang Daniel a song.

"When grown-ups are too busy to play with you, look around, look around, to find something to do!"

Daniel looked around his house for something to take to the Enchanted Garden. He found Tigey, paper, and crayons to draw with.

Mom Tiger picked up her tool kit, and off they went to the Enchanted Garden. On Trolley, Mom and Daniel sang together.

"We're on our way to work today, there is so much to do.
Won't you ride along with me? Ride along!
Won't you ride along with me?"

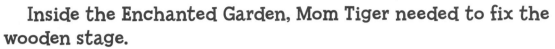

Inside the Enchanted Garden, Mom Tiger needed to fix the wooden stage.

"It looks like a railing broke," she said.

"And there's a hole in the stage too," said Daniel.

Luckily, his mom had brought new planks of wood to patch it up. "Can I help you fix the stage?" Daniel asked.

"Not this time, Helper Tiger," she said. "This is a grown-up job."

Daniel wondered what he should do while his mom was working.
He looked around and found his crayons and paper.
    "I know!" Daniel said. "I'm going to draw a picture of my mom!"

After he finished drawing, he wondered what else he could do. "I know!" Daniel said. "Let's make believe Tigey and I are carpenters, just like my mom!"

Daniel showed his mom his picture.
"I see," his mom said, smiling. "But now I have to get back to work," she told him.

Mom knew Daniel could find something else to do on his own until she was done.

Daniel sang another song.

"When grown-ups are too busy to play with you, look around, look around, to find something to do!"

Daniel looked around and found some empty boxes that his mom said he could use. "Hey, I think I found something else to do!"

He used his crayons to draw on the boxes. Then he turned the boxes into a rocket ship. He climbed inside and pretended to blast off into outer space. "Three . . . Two . . . One . . . Blast off!"

Then Daniel found more supplies to use. He wondered what he should build next. "I know!" he said. "This is an ice-skating pond!"

Soon Mom Tiger was finished working.

"Mom, look!" Daniel told her. "I made an ice-skating pond!"

"You found so much to do while I was busy," his mom said. "I'm so proud of you."

A few minutes later Mom Tiger showed Daniel how she had fixed the railing and patched the hole in the stage. "Wow, you really can do anything, Mom!" Daniel said.

"Thank you." His mom smiled. "Now, who wants to go ice-skating with me?"